Penelope

Countess of Arcadia

a play by

Helena Hann-Basquiat

illustrations by Ali Akbar

dilettante publishing

Penelope – Countess of Arcadia

Copyright © 2015, Helena Hann-Basquiat
Illustrations Copyright © 2015, Ali Akbar
Used by kind permission
All rights reserved.
ISBN 13: 978-0-9940419-4-4
ISBN 10: 0-9940419-4-2

Published in Canada by Dilettante Publishing

For Bill

No one writes them like they used to so I might as well try.

.

Prologve

Penny had been crying for three hours straight and I knew well enough to let her be. Penny isn't the type to cry unless her heart is truly broken. The fact that this was the second time it had been broken by the same person had put me in a truly ugly frame of mind, and I had already begun plotting the downfall of the young woman known in Casa de Hann-Basquiat only as the Empress. We do not speak her name anymore, especially after the events of last spring, when she lied first to Penny and then to the entire student committee to which Penny belonged. You may recall Penny calling for the Empress' head on a stick, and quite frankly, darlings, she deserved it. She deserved a reckoning of truly Shakespearean proportions...

Argument

The Countess Penelope of Arcadia, my very favourite niece, was the financial officer of the Society of the University of Arcadia. Nearly a year before, a group of students had been kicked out of the Society for misconduct. But then they began to publicly slander via the book of Face, the members of the committee, the Countess Penelope included.

Justice (and the vote of committee) declared that they should have been expelled. Instead, the Empress, weak-minded fool that she is, caved to the pressure of petitions and politics and invited them back into the Society, all sins forgiven. However, she acted without the support or authority of the rest of the committee and made this invitation in secret. Penelope found out about this and confronted the Empress privately, only to have the Empress deny all knowledge of the invitation. However, Penelope had proof by way of email that the Empress had indeed committed these foul deeds and did confront her in the assembly of the rest of the committee.

I had very much wished to continue this story by

telling you that the Empress had been removed from her station, or maybe even that she'd been drawn and quartered, or forced to clean the toilets of Grand Central Station with her tongue, or some other fitting punishment. I'd very much love to tell you that Penelope quit the society, flipped them the bird, and told them that if they needed her help, they could go fornicate with themselves. It would make a much finer, more emotionally satisfying tale if I could relate to you how the offenders were denied membership in the Society, were indeed expelled from the school, and were all now working at the local workhouse, regretting their immaturity. It would be a lovely tale, darlings, but I wouldn't want to lie to you. I'm guilty of many things, but I'm not a liar. At least, not when it counts.

No, the truth is, this committee was populated by the very young, and often the very young lack the mettle to do what is right, because sometimes doing what is right is unpopular. Or perhaps it is their youthful lack of confidence – fear that they would be doing the wrong thing. Who knows? Whatever the case, there was a lot of talk, but at the end of the day, nothing was done, the Empress kept her position, and Penelope, in fact, was coaxed back with desperate pleas, and sweet, trusting soul that she was, went back.

But the Empress, it seems, did not forget. Nearly a year has passed and young Penelope has gratefully left that world behind and good riddance. But as villains often do, the Empress lay in wait to exact her vengeance and an opportunity has, unbeknownst to Penelope, just arisen.

Now to fair Arcadia, where we lay our scene.

Caſt of Characterſ

Penelope

Countess of Arcadia.
A university student. After reading Alice in Wonderland during a particularly bad citric acid trip, Penny developed a penchant for dressing in outlandish striped socks and crinolines and enjoys turning her hair into sculptured works of art that require a scholarly knowledge of both Salvador Dali and Dr. Seuss to understand and/or appreciate.

Helena

Penelope's fiercely protective aunt. To make up for a crippling sense of high self-esteem, she dabbles in whatever she can get her hands into in order to fail spectacularly at something. Even theatre.

The Empreſſ Claudia

Empress of the Society of the University of Arcadia. Conniving and manipulative, she'll not be blamed for anything and will not admit to any wrong-doing, even if she is caught with her sticky little hands in the cookie jar.

Geneuieue

A moneylender. A greedy pinch-thrift who does not forgive debts and has been known to exact terrible consequences upon those in default.

Dante a member of the Society and friend to Penelope. He is a scholar and a poet and is in a fiery relationship with *Beatrice*, also a friend to Penelope. Neither has any love for the Empress.

Gadgette

An Inspector at
the University
of Arcadia.
A shrewd,
clever,
suspicious man,
who takes
justice very
personally.

Yorrick

A messenger who sells his services and has no loyalties one way or the other.

𝑌 𝑜 𝑣 - the audience, who feels it necessary to interject when it is completely inappropriate, destroying the illusion by breaking the fourth wall. What the fuck, You?

ACT I

Scene I

A tavern. Outside it is pouring rain. The Empress waits in a booth in the back corner of the room. Genevieve enters, soaking wet and annoyed.

Genevieve

Gods!
'Tis fine weather thou hast called me out in
And surely I am chill-ed to the bone!

Empress

The rain is but a gift from God. Thou can'st
Not pin foul weather on my blameless breast
Like a plague cross, nor hold me in debt for
Sickness incurred due to your improper
Preparation. Thou art no fool – thou know'st
A grey sky from blue.

Genevieve

I came not to blame thee for the rain nor
Petition thee for sunshine. I come for
What is owed and shall have it, else you face my wrath.

Empress

Surely thou speak'st of the bit of coin
You believe thou art due.

Genevieve

'Tis no bit of coin, thou sanctimonious,
Flap-mouthed, maggot pie! It is a small prize
And thou hast given me promises of
Reimbursement, sworn on the blood of thine
Own mother.

Empress

I promised no such thing! I told you most
Assuredly that our society
Could not bear such a debt.

Genevieve

Mark me,
Thou mangled, hedge-born, promise-breaker!
I have given thee time most ample and
Sufficient and my kindness has become
Like an ancient pair of breeches. I tire
Of your tongue-wagging and cannot bear the
Sight of thee. Thy dress is like a dog's breakfast!

Empress

Well, in truth, I did not choose these garments

Myself! I was in a rush to meet you
And my aide did, in haste, dress me in these
Most unseemly vestments.

Genevieve

I care not a tick!
Only where is my money that thou hast
Promis-ed? My garden is already quite well
Fertilized. I've no need for any more
Compost from thy putrid lips.

Empress

Methinks I need some air.

Genevieve

Methink'st thou art a general offence and
Every man should beat thee. [1] Be off then and
Get some air. T'would be unwise to run and
Prudent to return with what thou owest.

Empress

A moment then. I'll not flee, thou hast my word.

Genevieve

A valueless thing, broken and bespoiled.
Go, thou saucy, crook-pated, malt worm,
Before my angry foot finds purchase in
The enormous mounds of thy bottom.
Tempt not too much the hatred of my spirit,

---

[1] All's Well That Ends Well, Act II Scene III, William Shakespeare

For I am sick when I do look on thee. [2]

Empress exits to side stage

Empress

Am I a fool that I must contend with
Such nonsense that seems bound and determined
To dull my wits and ebb my strength? To have
Insults hurled upon me like an ass, when
I should have respect and all forms of duty?
Was it not I who, with demonstrations
Of mercy, did allow those charged with
Petty disobediences to rejoin
Their brethren in the bosom of our fair
Society? Aye, 'twas none but I did
Open arms and forgive. Now I find myself
With hounds nipping at my heels. But watch,
As I shall run quicker, smarter, and faster
And show you all that this fox is clever
And will not be caught. A ruthless creature, I,
And not afraid of spilling a little blood.
The Countess! I hate the Countess and she
Shall serve. When the hounds come sniffing 'round,
I shall wound her, and they cannot help but
Follow that scent to where she lies bleeding.
I shall form a trap so complete that she
Will not fail to step in't. And the yips
Of pain and the look of fear in her eyes
Will be the sweet cream I pour over my
Berries for dessert and vengeance shall stain
My smiling lips.

---

[2] A Midsummer Night's Dream, Act II Scene I, William Shakespeare

Genevieve

Hast the air consumed thee, thou poxy cur?
Or hast thee, with thy dull wits, lost the way?
Doth thou need a map to find thy way back?
Or should I send a rescue party hither
To fetch thee, thou errant dog?

Empress

I come, anon!
The air hast cleared my clouded mind and it
Doth occur to me to double mine efforts
To locate the missing funds. Surely something
Hath gone amiss, as thou hast ascertained,
And I shall check the Society ledger,
For indeed I hath promised recompense
To your fair self and I am no liar.

Genevieve

No liar? Then thou art a broken clock
That never ceases chiming the hour,
Ringing the same song in my weary ears.

Empress

I only mean to say that if there hath
Been an error in accounting, the fault
Lies not with me, good lady, but with she
Who held the books. *(Aside)* That foul-mouthed tart with
The stryp-ed socks and multi-coloured hair
Who dared call me liar in front of the
Entire assemblage. I'll not take the blame
When, with a little work, the sin can be
Lain at her feet. Before this day is done,
Mark my words, I'll see her blood in the street.

Genevieve

Thou art to blame for naught, t'would appear, for
Thy protestations art the mewling of
Kittens that win the heart of the genteel
Farmer and are spared drowning. Very well.
Bring me such proof as shall vindicate and
If a treasure I cannot collect, I
Will take my fee in a measure of flesh.
But 'ware me, Empress – should all thy
Explorations leave thee empty-handed –
I promise that t'will be thy hands I take
As my reward.

Exit Genevieve.

Empress

And thee I shall call villain! 'Twill be thy
Claws that leave their mark when the Countess,
Who wears naïveté like that curs-ed
Shirt of hers (the one that reads Fuckest Thee,
Thou Fucking Fuck), doth inquire as to whom
Hath delved into her affairs and made
Accusations of misappropriation.
Then shall I whisper into her eager ears
Of thy insurmountable greed and avarice
And extend a hand of equally
Offended friendship so she canst not then
Doubt I am no villain. I shall play
The innocent dove, come to warn her of
Danger, and vow to follow her into
The dragon's mouth. But in following her,
I do follow mine own dark ends. For when
The dragon doth open its fiery jaws,
'Twill not be the charry beast's fearsome teeth
The Countess will feel piercing her foolish

Breast, but mine own dagger, sharpened and
Envenom'd. And still I shall declare my
Innocence. I know not how, but surely
There is some poor fool that I can rake 'cross
The coals 'til his skin be like the Moor
At midnight – while I remain pure as
Freshly-fallen snow. But soft! The rain doth break
And there is much mischief to attend to!

Exit.

Scene II

A living room.
The Countess Penelope of Arcadia and her aunt Helena are watching the exploits of Cummerbund Bandersnatch and that fellow from The Hobbit.
But Helena, *thou sayest,* is not yon Cummerbund Bandersnatch also a player in Peter Jackson's cinematic masturbation to which thou hast already made reference?
Verily, I say unto you, I am the narrator here. Dost thou wish for the play to continue? Then kindly close thy gob lest the flies discover a new breeding bed in your open gorge, darling, and spread their insectile ejaculate all over thy unbridled tongue.
Where was't I? Ah yes. Sherlock...

Penelope

Loik, dost thou fink that Cummerbund is
'Appy wif 'is lady love? It doth break
Me bleedin' 'eart it doth. Loik, cheerio an' such.

Helena

Truly thou art an urchin, darling,
That thou would'st speak in such a
Dickensian manner when 'tis quite
Difficult indeed to maintain a
Dialogue most Shakespearean. Would that
You would'st drop the chimney sweeper facade
And regale me most clearly with news of
Thy plans for the future.

Penelope

'Tis not the future which findeth me fretful,
Fair Helena, but the present. I am
Ill at ease and fear that some foul news doth
Even now make its way hence to darken
Our doorstep.

Helena

Hast thou, perhaps by accident or good
Intentions gone afoul, caused some unseen
Offence that thou hast hid from me?

Penelope

No.

Helena

Thou art sure?

Penelope

No.

Helena

No, thou art not sure, or dost thou repeat
The insistence that thou hast not caused offence?

Penelope

The first one, thou prattling cockinjay!
I cannot be certain, for how can I
Delve into the minds of others and know
What offence I may have caused? Perhaps 'tis
Merely that I have shot my arrow o'er
The wall innocently, but, unaware,
Have wounded a dear sister. Ah! Cruel fate!

Helena

When was't thou hast taken up the practice of
Archery, darling?

Penelope

'Tis a metaphor, thou imbecilic,
Fawning coxcomb!

Helena

I do not fawn and hardly think that
Vanity is my sin.

Penelope

Thou most certainly dost, and 'tis surely
Thy most prevalent sin, though certainly
It doth not stand alone upon the stage.
'Tis like unto the demons our good Lord
Cast into the herd of swine. 'Tis Legion.

Helena

Bitch.

Penelope

Mewling, swag-bellied flax-wench!

Helena

Once more, thou dankish, beef-witted pignut!

Penelope

Thou art a mewling, swag-bellied flax wench.
Thy mother dropped thee on thy head to
Improve upon thy unseemly looks!

Helena

Strumpet!

Penelope

Dilettante!

Helena

Oh no, thou did'st not! Your virginity
Breeds mites, much like a cheese. [3]

Penelope

Wouldst thou stoop so low, thou cruel woman?
Then bring thy best, lest you have reason to
Say after I trounce thee, that thou hast held

---

[3] All's Well That Ends Well, Act I Scene I, William Shakespeare

Back on my account.

Enter Yorrick, a Messenger

Yorrick

Good and kindly Penelope, Countess
Of Arcadia! Good day to you, lady!

Penelope

And to you, sir. What is't thou hast need of?

Yorrick

I bring tidings from her ladyship, the
Empress.

Penelope

Empress Claudia?

Yorrick

The same, Countess.

Penelope

Fuck! 'Twould have been better for me today
If I had never been born! Better still
Had I just stayed in bed and explor'd the
Realms of self-pleasure whilst contemplating
The glorious voice of Lord Bandersnatch.

Yorrick

Yes, quite. But, my lady, I come bearing
A message, with all the trappings of friendship.

Penelope

I trust that degenerate woman's words
As I do adders fang'd. When it comes to
The crafting of lies, she is like the
Spider, which casts its web in friendly
Places in the sunshine, the clueless flies
To snare. In deception, she is skainsmate
To the Devil himself!

Yorrick

Aye, my lady, 'tis said she prefers the
Dish of male chicken the best, and doth
Consume her fill.

Penelope

Less art, sir, and more truth.

Yorrick

I speak no art, lady, and only tell the truth.

Penelope

Speak plainly then, good sir, and you shall have
My thanks.

Yorrick

I only mean to say that she is a
Real cock-gobbler, she is.

Penelope

Ah, yes. Very good. Thou art a fellow
Of infinite jest. If thou dost tire of

The life of a messenger, thou art quite
Suited to play the fool. Thou hast a
Letter for me then?

Yorrick

Yes, and I humbly take my leave.

Penelope

You cannot, sir, take from me anything
That I will more willingly part withal [4] —
Except my aunt. Wilt thou please take my aunt?
She is become most tedious, and I
Fear I grow murderous in her presence.

Helena

Penelope! You wound me!

Penelope

I do but jest!

Yorrick

You jest? For truly, your aunt is fair and
Comely. It would be my pleasure to relieve
You of the burden of her company.

Helena

Mark you, Penelope! It would be his pleasure.

---

[4] Hamlet, Act II Scene II, William Shakespeare

Yorrick

And thy pleasure, I assure you, sweet lady.

Penelope

All right, all right, away with you! Thou art
A dog with a bone, one which he wishes
To bury in soft and yielding soil. But
I assure you, the soil of my aunt
Helena is an unweeded garden
That goes to seed. Things rank and gross in
Nature possess it merely. [5]

Helena

Thou art damned, Penelope, and I will
Be the one that stops your foolish,
Odiferous breath.

Penelope

My breath doth not stink.

Helena

'Tis like a carrion dog, which breeds
Maggots in the hot sun.

Penelope

I choose to ignore you, lest you get a
Knock on thy head.

---

[5] Hamlet, Act I Scene II, William Shakespeare

Helena

What is't the Empress hath sent you hither?

Penelope

I know not, do I? I have yet to
Unfold this letter. I would have thought a
Telephone call simpler.

Helena:

'Tis true, darling, but a voice-over is
A convention more fitting for the
Cinema and, as this is a play, would
Only be off-putting the audience
Yonder.

Penelope

Dost thou speak of that roguish, rough-hewn
Congregation of sheep-fuckers there?

Helena

The same. And as we are the minstrels of
Their only entertainment, it serves that
We present the words of the Empress in
A way that suits the medium.

Penelope

As you like, then. I'll not engage in a
Battle of wits with thee, as thou stand'st
Ungirded. You read it.

Helena

(Reading letter) "My dearest compatriot, the most
Beautiferous Penelope–"
Beautiferous? 'Tis a vile phrase. 'Tis not
Even a real word, I'd wager. *(Reading letter)* "My trusted
Adviser and keeper of the coin of
The Society." She doth go on with
More titles and praise. Shall I continue
Or skip to the matter?

Penelope

What is the matter?

Helena

Nothing. What is the matter with you, lady?

Penelope

The matter she doth write in the letter.
The content, if it please you.

Helena

(Reading letter) "It doth pain me to write you thusly" –
Thusly? Doth she jest? Only the worst sort
Of couche-tard would'st use the word *thusly!* But
Pray you be patient, Countess, I shall be
Faithful and continue. *(Reading letter)* "but I have caught
Whiff of a foul wind –" Methinks she hath been
Downwind of thy breath, dear Penelope.

Penelope

Hand me the letter, thou infectious
Canker-blossom! *(Reading letter)* "The vile moneylender,

Genevieve, hath called upon me to account
For some small sum of money she claims she
Is owed, and like the eagles that peck at
The liver of the Titan Prometheus,
She returns every day to beg for what
I do not have. I call to thee, dear sister,
To aid me in proving that we are blameless
In any wrongdoing. She seeks the
Destruction of us all, I fear, and I
Am at a loss for how I ought to proceed.
I pray that thou art as wise as I believe
And that thou hast kept good record of the
Society coin. In this I trust our
Salvation. I have called a meeting with
All concern-ed parties and thy presence
Is required most urgently. If ever
You bore me any ill will, please let us
Bury our contention in the deep earth
Of forgiveness, and embrace again as
Sisters. Only together can we stand
Against such wanton greed and villainy.
I do not stand above you, dear sister.
The Society hath granted me the
Title of Empress, but I am ever
Your servant. Should I be of any help
To you, you need only ask."

Helena

Is that the end?

Penelope

She doth offer me a myriad of
Salutations, each one more sickly sweet
Than the next, like the buffet choices of
A gluttonous sugar-fiend.

Helena:

'Tis a trap.

Penelope

To be certain.
No fool, I. Though I oft' dress in motley, be not deceived.
Should she say the sky is blue, I should not take her word.
Her words fall unto an empty room and are not believed.
I will have more proof ere trust what I have heard.
Yon Empress would not recognize fair Honesty should
She pass him on the street,
Nor even if he had her legs 'round his back and his mouth
Upon her breast,
Such is her ignorance of the very concept so complete.
She doth whore herself to liars, sycophants, and all the rest
And when she hath had her fill of their corrupting seed,
She'll save the poisonous putrescence in crystal vessels,
Distilled unto a perfect rot,
Then serve it to some unsuspecting scapegoat upon her
Hour of need,
And the poor bleating creature is led to slaughter as her
Own sins are forgot.
But mark - I fear a suit of goatskin is being prepared for
Me e'en now,
And I must take action else I lose my head, although I
Know not how.

Helena

Thou know'st how she did deceive you in the past.

Penelope

I do indeed. But let me not think on't.

Helena

'Twas in the late mid-winter and the ground
Was barely thaw'd—

You

But, Helena, flashbacks are really
Something of a cinematic convention
As well. That is to say, thou did'st give the
Countess Penelope grief about the
Idea of a telephone conversation,
But now thou dost begin to reminisce
About events nearly a year past. Thou
Art not Orson Welles and this, clearly, is
Not Citizen Kane, for unless mine eyes
Deceive me, there is nary a snow globe
In sight, and the word *rosebud* hath not
Escaped thy lips.

Helena

I must set the scene, thou interfering
Rogue! Speak to me not of conventions, for
I pride myself in forms most unconventional.
I spit out convention like a scrap of
Beef or a bit of underdone potato,
Lest I be visited by ghosts of
Business partners long dead.

You

Didst thou, in truth, make a completely
Esoteric and random Dickens
Reference just now?

Helena

I did, scoundrel, and I pray you pardon
Me, or else, if not, find some wet hole and
Fornicate with thyself. Now let me get
Back to the play. The play's the thing, in which
I'll catch the conscience of the Empress.

You

Well, if thou art planning on cribbing lines
From Hamlet, thou should'st at the very least
Try to be faithful to the text.

Penelope

Well, it didn't, loik, *rhyme*, did it? Ennit an' such.

Helena

Thank you, darling.
'Twas late mid-winter and the ground was barely thaw'd,
And Claudia did fancy herself above the common throng.
Elevating herself just a hair's breadth lower than a god,
She hired minstrels to immortalize her lofty works in song.
In truth, she was full of fear and weak as a helpless child.
Whenever questioned she would always deflect blame,
For fear of losing power of which she'd become beguiled.
Truth be told she was the Empress but in name,
And yet she took upon herself to free the malcontents
Without the fair agreement or the council of her peers,
And lied to the Countess, which made not a lick of sense.
For Penelope gave documents confirming all her fears
To her Society compatriots, who looked with chilly dread
As Penelope cried havoc and called for the Empress' head.

Penelope

And yet her head remains safely on her
Weak, shrugging shoulders. I fear nothing can
Be well as long as she draws breath and that
All will be ill.

Helena

Methink'st 'tis safe to assume that she draws
Breath still. Is't too much to hope she draws this
Breath in Hell?

Penelope

If she draws breath then nothing can be well.

Helena

What is't you would have me do? Shall I fill
Her bed with snakes?

Penelope

And what would that accomplish, but to bed
Her down with kin? No, I must discover
How much mischief she has already caused,
Though I fear the worst: that all my records
Have been destroyed, or else doctored to ensure
That even I cannot help but look
Upon them and declare me guilty.

Helena

What wilt thou do?

Penelope

Lady, I know not.

Exeunt.

Scene III

A common room where members of the Society do their business.
Beatrice and Dante are there, discussing the Nine Circles of Hell.

Dante

And then that dizzy-eyed, Italian
Clack-dish hath called me a bootless, milk-livered varlet!

Beatrice

What did'st thou then, pray tell?

Dante

What choice had I, sweet lady, but to
Follow yon poet Virgil into the
Depths of Hell?

Beatrice

Thou liest!

Dante

Only with thee, I swear, lest dogs pull this
Tongue from its bony cage.

Beatrice

Take care, thou roguish flatterer, else you
Sleep with dogs tonight. Thou surely knowest
What is said about them that lie with dogs.

Dante

Hast thou no patience, woman? I shall get
To the Seventh Circle anon and will
Tell you all about what happens to them
That lie with dogs.

Beatrice

I only referred to the adage about
Dogs and fleas.

Dante

'Twould be best to flee, if the dog in question
Were that currish, dog-hearted wench what calls
Herself the Empress.

Beatrice

She is a churlish, ill-bred wagtail, that one,
And Hell is too good for her sort. Did'st thou
Hear how she did'st cower like a frightened
Bird when our lady the Countess did question
Her in the court?

Dante

In the end, she did'st sweep the whole affair
Under the bed like a lazy, toad-spotted
Chambermaid.

Beatrice

Not that she hath ever done the work of
A chambermaid.

Dante

Not her, no. And if by chance she hath, by
Some strange accident, been caught cleaning, why,
I swear by all the stars that she would throw
A mewling babe to the wolves afore
Taking blame for something so below her
Adopted station.

Beatrice

Damnable bitch! What Circle dost thou put
Her in then? Do tell.

Dante

Well, not Limbo, the first Circle. 'Twas not
A horrible enough fate for our
Conniving, flap-mouthed miscreant of an
Empress. Limbo was filled with virtuous
Souls, of which she is none. If I am honest,
Sweet Beatrice, 'twas a place I could linger,
Full of green fields and a castle of seven
Doors, where dwelt the wisest men of history.

Beatrice

Well, go on then. Get thee to back Hell, thou
Idle-headed knave! For I've no need of
Thee in my bed if the best use of thy
Tongue thou can'st think of is to wag it on
About how lovely art the fields of Limbo.

Dante

I would, dear lady, were it not for the
Neighbouring circles which, if thou canst but
Believe it, would be a trial more difficult
To endure than even thy piggish snoring.
True, the smell of brimstone would be a welcome
Change to thy breath in the morn, but thy soft
And yielding flesh is enticement enough
To keep me by thy side, foul breath be damned.

Beatrice

Methink'st thou wilt not find my flesh so
Yielding, sirrah.

Dante

Oh, thou knowest thou art an angel by
Day and a devil by night. 'Tis why I
Love thee so.

Beatrice

Thou art a goat, both rank and reeky, and
Bleat as thou might, thou shalt have none of me,
For thy words are artless and cruel. 'Tis
Only lust thou speak'st of, not love.

Dante

You wound me, lady! For thee I would face
The storm of the Second Circle of Hell,
Reserved for those carnal malefactors whose
Lusty appetites hath run away with
Their reason. I am no Tristan, fair lady,
And you, no Isolde.

Beatrice

Nay, nor Romeo and Juliet.

Dante

To the very word, my lady. Thou art
The desire of my bosom.

Beatrice

Methink'st tis my bosoms thou desire'st.

Dante

'Tis true they are magnificent. Like two
Kittens wrestling 'neath a coverlet.

Beatrice

Truly, thou art a poet.

Dante

Thou mockest me, but I love thee still.

Beatrice

Did'st thou see the like of our foul Empress

In this Second Circle? Do you find her fair?

Dante

Neither fair nor honest. And no, Lust is
Not our Empress' sin, leastways not the main.
For I know not a man who finds her comely
Nor have I seen her look kindly at a
Woman.

Beatrice

What, then? What lies 'neath the fleshy surface
Of the Second Circle?

Dante

Why, Circles Three, Four and Five, of course,
Directly followed by the Sixth and Seventh,
Which did indeed contain the sort that
Preferred intercourse with creatures feathered
And furry, as well as an entire
Congregation of vile and wicked men:
Murderers and blasphemers, and suicides
And wastrels. But thou art no fool and must
Surely have an understanding of matters
Mathematical. Am I telling thee
Aught which thou did'st not already ascertain?

Beatrice

Thou art a tedious, hasty-witted
Clotpole and I know not why I entertain
Thy nonsense.

Dante

Perhaps 'tis the size and skill of my clotpole.

Beatrice

Is there nary a man who is not in
Love with his own, nor indeed, any man
Who doth not flatter himself a master
In the bedchambers, with naught but his own
Testimony in his favour?

Dante

My, thou art a saucy, common-kissing
Giglet! 'Tis the Eighth Circle of Hell for
Thee, slanderer! And thou would'st be in the
Good company of that fly-bitten wench
The Empress.

Beatrice

Ah, so! The door is finally opened.

Dante

And just as quickly closed, I fear. For hark!
Here comes our lady, the Countess. How fare
Thee, lady?

Enter Penelope

Penelope

My back acheth in anticipation
Of the blade. My mouth is dryer than a
Kitten's litter and tastes about the same.

Dante

Pardon, my lady, forget I spoke.

Beatrice

A kitten's litter? 'Tis a foul metaphor.

Dante

'Tis a simile, thou beslubbering
Illiterate. That she doth use the
Qualifier "than a" denotes the phrase
Most surely as a simile. And thou
Say'st I am artless.

Beatrice

No, I hath said that thou art without heart. Thy
Tongue is sharper than thy wit, and hath cut
Me too often.

Penelope

Forgive me, Dante, is't? And fair Beatrice.
I meant no offence. What is't you were
Discussing before I arrived?

Beatrice

The Nine Circles of Hell, where the punishment
Is divided by category,
According to the sin, Greed, Gluttony,
Pride, Lust, Sloth, Wrath and Envy being chief
Amongst them.

Penelope

The Seven Deadly Sins. Yes, as mentioned
In that film with Morgan Freeman.

Dante

The one with the penguins? Or speak'st thou of
The film where Jim Carrey is awarded
The powers of the Almighty and doth
Perform unnecessary calibration
On Jennifer Aniston's breast size?

Penelope

Methink'st 'tis the one where the penguins join
Up with Robin of Locksley to defeat
Alan Rickman before he doth go on
To perform the Avada Kedavra
Spell and kill Bruce Willis at the end of
The fifth *Dieth Hard, Harry Potter* film.
What was the nature of thy discussion?

Beatrice

Only philosophical, I assure you.
Perhaps a touch spiritual, I
Do confess, but certainly nothing
Physical hath occurred betwixt us.

Penelope

No, I mean, wherefore art thou discussing
Such infernal matters, and in what context?

Dante

I had (however erroneously)
Offended my dear lady by conceding
That Limbo was not, in truth, a terrible
Place, but that I could not bear staying there,
In part because I would miss her dearly.

Beatrice

Thou did'st never…

Dante

And in part because of what lieth below
Limbo. We spoke of the fate of the lusty
In some small detail, but only touched
Upon the fate of the greedy and
Gluttonous, the wrathful and the heretics.
We did make some brief mention of the fate
Of the violent, who are punish-ed
By fire and blood, and then I believe we
Had arrived at the gate of Geryon,
The wing-ed dragon with the face of an
Honest man but the sting of the scorpion's tail.

Beatrice

My lord doth believe that he has been shown
A vision of Hell and, led by the poet
Virgil, did plumb its depths. I had, in jest,
Inquired upon his opinion on the
Fate of our good Empress.

Penelope

O sweet perdition! Whatever vision
Of torture or damnation thou hast received,
'Tis a far, far better fate than she deserves,
Than what I would have done; it is a far,
Far better rest that she goes to than I
Would have her ever know.

You

Did'st thou just truly crib Sidney Carton's

Parting lines from Dickens' *Tales of Two Cities?*
Hast thou not already pilfered enough
From the dead?

Helena

I'm not even here, darling. To whom dost
Thou address thy complaint?

Penelope

Ye gods!
A thousand pardons, good Dante, kindly Beatrice.
I pray you – continue.

Dante

Flatterers, liars and thieves, seducers
Of men – all find their home in the Eighth Circle
Of Hell, as will our good Empress, for where
But in a lake of boiling pitch doth a
Politician with sticky fingers belong?
I pray she doth also spend a spell
Immersed in human excrement, the
Prescribed punishment for flatterers.

Penelope

I fear she hath laid for me a snare
Upon which I cannot help but step.

Beatrice

At that she doth excel. Perhaps 'tis her
Only gift, besides escaping blame.

Penelope

She doth dangle the carrot with the stick
In plain view, and yet I cannot ignore
Her summons, lest she hang me even in
My absence.

Dante

Then why, lady, dost thou linger here when
Clearly thou ought be elsewhere, responding
To this summons?

Penelope

I come in search of a book.

Beatrice

I assure you there is nothing of
Interest here, dear Countess, save for a
Half-dozen tattered paperbacks with
Scandalous covers. Perhaps the library
Might afford you more options.

Penelope

I seek a specific book.

Dante

Not likely, my lady. Nothing here on
That subject. Nor the Atlantic, I'd wager.

Penelope

I seek my ledger. 'Tis my salvation.

Dante

Let not the priest hear you say that or it'll
Be the Sixth Circle and a flaming tomb
For thee, thou heretic!

Beatrice

If I can be of assistance, good lady,
My hands are thine.

Dante

But the rest of her doth rest in my hands,
Lest you forget.

Penelope

'Tis been an age since I set foot in this
Space, but surely my ledger should be
Safely where I hath left it.

Beatrice

Wherefore dost thou search for that which surely
Thou hast no need of? Thou hast left the
Society months hence.

Penelope

It appeareth that my honour hath been
Impugned and I am under some degree
Of investigation.

Dante

Ah, how troubling! A dear friend of mine
Hath been, as of late, under investigation.

Beatrice

By whom? What friend is't?

Dante

Never mind whom, thou troublesome hen.
And by whom dost thou think? By an ill-tempered
Physician, who did prod him terribly.

Beatrice

But why a doctor? Seems utterly queer
That he would be investigated by
A doctor.

Dante

Too many trips to the nunnery.

Penelope

Devout was he?

Dante

Devout and penniless.

Beatrice

Bless his heart.

Dante

'Twas not that type of nunnery, Beatrice,
My love. 'Twas the other kind.

Beatrice

You mean?

Dante

Poor sod's poker rotted clean off in the
Fire of some pox-marked strumpet's cunny-hole.
Now we call 'im Half-Jack.

Beatice

Why's that then?

Penelope

Why, 'cause 'is name were Jack, ennit? Now 'es
'Alf Jack. Am I right?

Dante

Thou speakest true, good Countess.

Beatrice

I wish I had more luck, lady, but
Ever since the Empress did'st clean out this
Room three days ago, I have not been able
To find my own shadow. 'Twas passing strange,
Her doing it herself. I have it on
The word of her chambermaid that she hath
More in common with a barnyard rat than
Just her charm.

Dante

She is slovenly, my lady. I hath
Found things strange and wondrous underneath these

Carefully tidied furnishings that thou dost
Now see before thee, whose usual state
Doth resemble a dig for a Pharaoh's tomb.

Beatrice

'Tis true, my lady. Methink'st the cure for
Canker-blossoms hath, until late, been growing
In that corner now behind thee, which now
Could'st serve as a table for us to dine.

Penelope

I am fuck'd. Surely I hath my legs bent
Back and am, even now, enjoying a
Cigarette post-coital.

Dante

Do go on.

Beatrice

Lady, thou hast lost me. I do not follow.
Lead me, so that I may see.

Penelope

It is as I feared, and she hath beat me
To my only hope. Now could I drink hot
Blood and do such bitter business as the
Day would quake to look on. [6]

Beatrice

Art thou certain you wouldn't rather a

---

[6] Hamlet, Act III Scene II, William Shakespeare

Nice cuppa tea?

Penelope

Mark me – I'll not ignore this coincidence,
And pray that no wise man could do the same.
The Empress think'st that she hath unarm'd me,
By removing all traces of my
Honest accounting, but she hath all the
Brazen hubris of a wolf that doth leave
Its pack, unable to think of the whole
And cannot, in her reasoning, find
Value in friendship. Fie! It is a
Pestilence on her skin, the very word
Like bitter wine in her mouth, and she hath
Spit so many out between her lying
Lips that she doth not see her cup is dry.
She hath valued her own treachery too
Dearly and undervalued my own
Honest reputation. She hath crushed the
Grapes of wrath too hastily, fermenting
Them into a sour, bitter, potent swill
And hath grown drunk and giddy, thinking
Herself victorious. I will hold fast
To a sweeter vintage, cultivated
With time and care. *In fermentum et veritas* –
The truth will out. And now I leave you, friends.
I thank you for your counsel. I am called
To council where I fear I must face my
Accusers. If thou see'st me not hereafter…

Dante

Avenge thy death without predjudice?

Beatrice

Tell thy aunt Helena thou lovest her?

Penelope

No, thou spleeny, swag-bellied joithead!
If thou see'st me not hereafter, do not
Forget to lock up after thou hast left.

Exeunt

ACT II

Scene I

The office of the Investigator. The Empress waits for Penelope and whispers lies into the Investigator's ears.

Gadgette

Thou hast brought me here, lady, and here I am.
What wilt thou have of me? And where, pray thee,
Is thy charge, the Countess of Arcadia?

Empress

Have mercy on her, I beg thee, for hath
We not all sinn'd and fallen short of the
Glory of God? If our Heav'nly Father
Can'st forgive, then surely thou, a mere man,
Can'st pardon such a lowly, pitiful
Creature. Or dost thou desire to be judged
By the same measure, should thy day of
Reck'ning come at the hands of mortal men?

Gadgette

My lady, I will do as my station commands.

Empress

In truth my heart doth ache for such as she.
For what dire needs, like starving babes, must be
Fed that she would'st rob her kin and kind? For
Is't that not what we were? If not by blood
Then by purpose and a commonality
Of spirit? Fie! I'll not think on't. It doth
Chill my blood to ponder elsewise – that she
Could have, with full malice, betrayed those self-same
Hands that did hold her up when she could not
Stand or wiped her brow in sickness or clasped
Her own in rejoicing.

Gadgette

My lady, I am not Saint Peter, nay,
Nor Osiris, to judge the living or
The dead. 'Tis not for me to took into
The heart of the Countess and say "Thou dost
Not measure up, thou fiend!" and cast her into
Darkness without end. I am here as a
Just and impartial observer merely,
To bear witness to thy complaint.

Empress

'Tis not my complaint, good sirrah! It is
Poison in mine ears to even hear the
Words that hath been spoke against her.

Gadgette

'Tis thy name on the record of complaint, lady.

Empress

Am I not thy Empress?

Gadgette

Not mine, my lady. Thou speak'st not for me or mine.

Empress

Thou errant, ill-nurtured puttock! Mind thy
Place or the buzzards wilt have thy tongue!

Gadgette

Thou dost bark at the wrong turn, thou foolish,
Weather-bitten bitch! Take a nip at me
And thou wilt find thyself tethered to a
Tree like a mad Irishman or a drunken
Dog. Thou hast no power here, 'tis best you
Remember.

Empress

My name, good sirrah, doth stand for our
Entire Society. 'Tis my burden
To bring forth this complaint, despite my
Reservations. And yet –

Gadgette

And yet?

Empress

And yet I hath heard such damning testimony
That in faith I cannot help but believe it.
From whom I cannot say, for as I hath

Already said, 'tis my burden.

Gadgette

Thou speak'st for the Society, 'tis
Understood. But if there is aught which needs
Be spoke by other voices –

Empress

Nay, thou can'st hold me at my word, for I
Bear the weight of this foul task. I must be
Strong. For if, when her sins are discovered,
Yon Countess doth fall into a sadness
And from that sadness into despair and
Then into rage – might she not, in her
Anger, seek vengeance on those who did, in
The name of honesty and truth and justice,
Shed light on her wrongdoings? Nay, I'll not
Have that on my conscience. If 'tis as I
Fear – that desperation hath led her to
Stray from her otherwise righteous path to
Tread this precarious new direction
On the very edge of folly, then I
Fear that this discovery may lead her, as
Off a cliff side, into madness. Should she,
In her fever, seek a target for her
Rage, 'twere best it be me.

Gadgette

Thou dost care for her?

Empress

As if she were my own flesh. 'Tis why the
Betrayal stings so and why I am so
Loathe to accept it. But Cain slew Abel

And surely they did'st nurse together at
Their mother's breast. Perhaps I am a fool
To believe that the love that I doth bear
The sweet Countess is requited.

Gadgette

'Tis no sin to trust thy kin and the Ninth
Circle of Hell awaits traitors. All things
Being equal, should she not be able
To reconcile thy tale with her own...

Empress

Fear breeds liars, surely thou know'st this.

Gadgette

As I know my name. But I know'st not how
To tie the hangman's collar, if't be thy
Intention that I condemn the Countess
On thy word alone.

Empress

No such thing was in my thoughts! But thou art
A man and the Countess hath charms and is
Passing fair. 'Tis easy to sort out lies
From the mouth of a viper, but when the
Selfsame falsehoods are spoken with lips that
Fill thy dreams with fantasies of pleasure,
The clouding of thy judgment is assured.

Gadgette

My lady, I am made of mettle
Steelier than this.

Empress

And yet thine eyes have been over every
Inch of me.

Gadgette

Impertinent wench!

Empress

I shall conceal myself, that I might hear
The extent of her falsity. Thou dost
Not need to lead her anywhere. Merely
Give the half-faced dewberry a sufficient
Length of rope and I warrant she wilt hang
Herself with't anon.

Gadgette

Go! Go! Get thee away then! The very
Sight of thee hath become intolerable
To mine eyes. Thou hast all the subtlety
Of a screaming gull and the guile of an
Egg-sucking fox. Get ye gone! The lady
Approacheth.

Exit the Empress, hiding herself in a wardrobe. Penelope enters

Penelope

'Tis here, in this pale sepulchre that I will meet my doom,
This lonely place so unfamiliar to mine eyes,
Far away from the cherished comfort of my home,
No Helena by my side to contradict their lies.
I am undone; 'tis written, sealed, tattooed upon my face.
And what sin hath I committed to deserve this cruel fate,
Save trusting overmuch and having lost sight of my place?

What recompense have I, her prideful appetite to sate?
Is this the price I pay for pulling on the tiger's tail?
No tiger, she doth, like a scorpion, hide and crawl,
An armoured thing that only plays at being frail
With tiny pricks she think'st to surely bring about my fall.
But more than irksome stings 'twill take,
This lion's heart to pierce;
For though I be but little, I am fierce. [7]

Gadgette

My lady, I await you within.

Penelope

What? All by thyself? Surely thou art joined
By the Empress and a meeting of my
Fellows of the Society.

Gadgette

Let us not, like territorial dogs,
Begin by sniffing our respective
Hindquarters, nor, like those fools o'erwhelmed by
Their own biology, engage in a
Meaningless game of measurement. I assur'st
Thee – mine is bigger by half than thine, and
If thou wilt not tug at mine, then I will
In turn leave thine to thy own free hand.

Penelope

What an excellent, honest knave thou art!
Very well, then. I come, anon. *(Aside)* Bring thy
Worst, thou fucking fickle Fates. There is naught

---

[7] A Midsummer Night's Dream, Act III Scene II, William Shakespeare

Thou cans't do to me that I hath not
Already resigned myself to.

Gadgette

My lady?

Penelope

I come, anon!

Gadgette

Excellent courage. Thou know'st why thou art here?

Penelope

My father, a man of exquisite taste
And powerful appetite, hath, in show
Of excellent judgment, found my mother
A wond'rous beauty, and did engage with
Her in acts, which they surely found most
Pleasurable, but which I'd rather expel
As far from my thoughts as east is from west.

Gadgette

Methink'st thou hast been watching thy dog hump
Thy neighbour's leg overmuch and it hath
Rotted thy brain, Penny.

Penelope

Thou art far too familiar, Inspector
Gadgette. My name is Penelope, or
Countess, if thou wish'st.

Gadgette

As thou wilt, lady. Thy impertinence
Dost thou no favours here. I am no
Enemy of thine.

Penelope

Just her hound. Tell me truly – doth she rub
Thy belly? Scratch those hard to reach places?
Give thee a bone? Even such as she must
Have some effect on thee, though she be as
Comely as an alley-born whey-face, and
Her hair doth, at best, bring to mind both the
Colour and odour of old dishwater.
Still, i'the dark, we are all but lumps of
Flesh and tender, soggy holes to explore,
Are we not?

Gadgette

A charmer, thou! And dost thou kiss thy
Mother with that selfsame sewer of a mouth?

Penelope

My mother hath been dead many years, my lord.
Thou bring'st me here for a purpose, did'st thou not?

Gadgette

Not I, good lady, though thou seem'st to call
Me villain where I am none.

Penelope

Your pardon, sirrah. This entire proceeding
Doth vex me, for 'tis not as I was told.

Where I expected conversation,
Instead I find investigation and,
I fear, condemnation without cause.

Gadgette

Not so, thou hast my word. I am but an
Arbiter and desire'st most powerfully
To hear thy tale, for all I hath heard thus
Far doth paint thee as, at best, a desperate
Thief and, at worst, a cold and callow
Villain with all the conscience of snake
As it devours its prey.

Penelope

Very well. What lies hath she told thee, that
I may best explain myself?

Gadgette

Thou'rt called to account for a great sum
That hath, according to the records in
My care, been paid by thee, though wherefore
I know not. 'Tis why thou standest before
Me here. Thou wert in command of the Society
Coin, and it is thy duty to make accounting.

Penelope

'Twas my duty, good sirrah, some months ago.
Surely thou know'st I am no longer
In that position.

Gadgette

Still, is this not thy name, signed here on
Several requisitions?

Penelope

'Tis indeed, and if that were damning
Evidence, then surely I did damn myself
Every time I did sign my own name. 'Twas
My duty, my lord.

Gadgette

Was't not also thy duty to account for
Every penny that thou did'st distribute?

Penelope

Indeed thou dost describe my post to the
Word, my lord. In what way hath I failed in
My duty? For surely that is why I
Am called here – to answer for some negligence
Or supposed willful act of pilferage,
Is't not?

Gadgette

Can'st thou account for all monies here
Upon this list?

Penelope

Give't me and I shall examine it
Most carefully. *(Reading)* "To the office of
Recreation, ten shillings... To the office
Of Health, five shillings... to the office of
Finance... fifty shillings." Oh, thou damn-ed
Fool! Thou beslubbering fool-born knave!
Hath I damned myself with my own pen, which
Doth indeed prove more fatal than the cutlass?

Gadgette

Tell me truly, wherefore pay'st thou thine own
Office? 'Tis queer indeed and doth offend
My sensibilities. 'Twere thought that truly
There is something rotten in the state of
Arcadia and thou art the cause.

Penelope

This doth appear passing strange, I confess,
But I assure you, 'twas all fair dealings,
And I hath accounted for every
Penny in my ledger.

Gadgette

Excellent lady! Thy protestations
Art most welcome. It would'st give me no pleasure
To see thee in chains. Where is't this ledger
Fine, that I might check the contents against
This list of mine?

Penelope

It hast, my lord, disappear'd. Where, I know
Not, though I surely hath suspicions.

Gadgette

'Tis most convenient, that the very thing
That might seal thy fate, or confirm the charges
Brought against thee hath suddenly vanish'd
Into the air like smoke.

Penelope

In truth I find it most inconvenient,

Sirrah, as I am innocent, and 'tis
The only scrap of proof I have – except
My good and honest word which, I can see
By thy furrowed brow, thou value'st as thou
Dost a scrap of fat.

Gadgette

I know'st thee not, young Countess, and thou hath
No credit with me. If thou say'st thou art
Innocent and the Empress doth believe
You to be guilty, then I'll have more proof
Than thy words ere I'll pass you to the hangman.

Penelope

What say'st thou? Dost mine ears deceive me?

Gadgette

'Tis not my place to judge the content of
Thy character, lady. 'Tis true that something
Is not quite right here, but thy honest
Disposition troubles me. I hath known
Many a guilty man who, when confronted
With his crimes, doth mewl and beg, or else, with
Indignant rage, deny his crimes outright.
Thou hast done neither. Instead, with reason
And wisdom, acknowledged the appearance
Of evil and hath not shied your eyes from
What is surely damning evidence.
And yet thou say'st there doth exist, though where
Thou know'st not, records that would expunge all
Guilt and ease my suspicious mind. I'll not
Be Pilate and wash my hands of thee that
The Empress might have her pound of flesh. I'll
Grant thee the benefit of doubt and look

Further into this matter.

Penelope

Excellent Inspector! I could kiss thy
Lips a thousand times!

Gadgette

And I would be the better for it. But
Thank'st me not too soon, for if this ledger
I cannot locate, or if 'tis not as
Thou say'st and the evidence falleth
Not in thy favour, I shall do my duty,
Though it vexeth my spirit to do so.

Penelope

Surely thou dost already realize
The ledger hast been destroyed. There is some
Purpose behind all this, I fear, more than
Just the Empress' well-known contempt for
Me. I shall know the truth of it and perhaps
This will be the path to my acquittal.

Gadgette

Good lady, I know not the root that hast
Brought forth this argument betwixt you and
That goatish horn-beast who calleth herself
Empress and, in truth, I care not. I hath
Lost nary a moment's rest in the
Consideration of't. But these
Circumstances are indeed curious.
Were I Penelope and you the
Inspector, what advice would'st thou offer me?

Penelope

Thou art a clever fellow, good Inspector.
Follow the money. 'Tis what I would'st
Advise thee, were thou the lovely and charming
Countess of Arcadia and I an
Errant Inspector. There's not a rascal
In all Arcadia such as thee and
Thou hast my thanks.

Gadgette

I hath done thee no favours, good lady.
Still, were I Penelope and I had
Questions about money, the first stop on
My quest would'st, without a doubt, be with that
Cullionly, unchin-snouted, pinchpenny
Genevieve. Whate'er coin doth pass through
Arcadia, 'tis said that she hath had the scent of it.

Penelope

I woulds't take my leave of thee, sirrah.
Methink'st that time be'st not my ally, and
That by lingering here I do myself
Disservice as well as thee. For if thou
Seek'st truth, then needs must that I go find
It for thee.

Gadgette

Thou canst, my lady, take from me what thou wilt.

Exit Penelope. Enter the Empress, from out of the wardrobe.

Empress

Thou poisonous, flap-mouthed maggot! I hath

Served that pig with crisped flesh, the apple
Firmly wedged in her snoutish maw, and thou
Hast not the manly gall to cut into
Her? Thou puking, cowardly foot-licker!

Gadgette

Methink'st thou doth require a candling of
Thine ears, for did I not tell you I am
No judge, nay, nor an executioner,
Though by the fiery tempest that doth storm
Behind thy eyes, 'twould seem that thou thinkest
Contrariwise.

Empress

I expect'st thee to do thy duty.
And punish the culprit of this foul deed.

Gadgette

And I shall. But 'tis not for the likes of
Thee to dictate my duty. Should I
Discover in my inquiries that thou
Hast brought false accusation against the
Countess, fear not her own reprisal, for
'Twill be my hand that does slap thee down like
I would a fly and pin thee in thy place.

Empress

Dost thou also fearlessly play with fire,
That thou would'st court destruction so? 'Tis
Well-known not to cross me, lest I find some
Deep hole to drop you in, over which I
Will roll a stone and erase thee from my
Memory. My yard hath several such holes
And stones, full of fools and dim-witted

Miscreants who did esteem themselves above
My reproach, and did'st not heed this dire
Lesson that I will, in kindness, impart
To thee anon – fuck'st thou not with me.

Gadgette

Again, I say go! Go! Darken not my
Door again, lest I turn my leery eye
Your way. I shall find the truth of this and
Report my findings back to thee with haste.
Until that day, forget my name. Would that
I could do the same for you, but alas,
It is like an earworm that hath burrowed
In my brain and made its unwelcome home
There. It doth prey upon me like an
Evil thing, and I fear I will never
Be rid of it or thee. Go! Get thee gone!

Empress

I go. The sight of thee doth cause my gorge to rise!

Exit the Empress

Gadgette

One taketh me for a fool, the other a fool doth take
But which is which, I truly cannot tell.
On paper, the Countess doth a guilty party make
But paper doth burn and cannot stand i'the court of Hell.
The Empress doth seem less concerned with truth
Than finding fault with young Penelope.
Methink'st she hath some cause to punish this poor youth
And believe'st she hath found her avenging weapon in me.
I'll not be used in such a crude and artless way
Nor play the game according to the Empress' rules

If either prove a liar, be assured I'll have my day
And cheerfully go to task at her with all available tools.
Whoe'er hath borne false witness shall pay a sinner's price
And the Hell to which I send her shall seem like Paradise.

Exit

Scene II

Genevieve's place of business — a den of usury and greed, where the desperate go in time of need and where Penelope hath gone seeking answers.

Penelope

Where art thou, you blood-sucking worm?

Genevieve

Hiding in plain sight 'twould appear, not that
I've any reason to avoid thee.

Penelope

Hast thou not? Then perhaps we might speak
Together without malice, for I hath
A great need and I believe thou art in
Possession of that which would quench my thirst.

Genevieve

Mistake not my lack of ire as friendship,
Thou callow, brazen-faced cow. If but half
Of what I've heard of thee is true, methink'st
Thou wilt have need of a friend like me
Before long. Money troubles, my lady?

Penelope

I would'st knock out all my teeth and sell
Myself to a nunnery ere I turn
To thee to solve my money troubles, thou
Bloated leech. But wait – who was't told thee I
Had money troubles? 'Tis wondrous strange that,
For I've no more worries than the next in
That regard.

Genevieve

O pardon me, good Countess. 'Tis my mistake.

Penelope

Thy sin's not accidental, but a trade. [8]

Genevieve

I trade in many things, lady, but not,
I fear, in gilly girls such as thee. Go
Ply thy sinful trade elsewhere. As thou can'st
See, I am a busy woman and have
No time for thy wicked tongue.

---

[8] Measure For Measure, Act III Scene I, William Shakespeare

Penelope

Thou art a shrewd woman, Genevieve, and
'Tis said thou know'st much of the affairs
Of Arcadia. Why, I hath heard it
Told that not a penny goes out of place
That thou dost not hear of it.

Genevieve

Hell hath its fill of flatterers, Countess.

Penelope

'Tis not flattery, lady, only ask
Thyself why I am here? Surely thou know'st.
If I am not here for money, then why?

Genevieve

Thou came'st here expecting to find me thy
Enemy, and now that thou see'st I
Am none, thou find'st thyself like the strange
Ouroboros, chasing a monster only
To catch your own tail in thy mouth. I am
No dragon, at least, not the dragon thou seek'st.

Penelope

What know'st thou of dragons?

Genevieve

I know they are hoarders of gold and that
They are not to be trusted. This one in
Particular is a poor, underfed
Lizard indeed and hath found herself in
My debt and hath not the funds to pay. 'Twere

Better she had Beezlebub himself
In her shadow than me. Methink'st thou know'st
Who I mean, for she hath, I believe, thrown
Thee to the dogs, thinking that by painting
Thee the villain, that I would find thee more
Attractive prey and pour my wrath out on
Thee instead of she.

Penelope

And was she mistaken?

Genevieve

I shall tell thee what I hath told that
Measly-faced worm – I want my money. 'Tis
No concern of mine the whys or wherefores,
Excuses or explanations. I hath
No desire to know the magician's secrets,
Nor do I crave to see the cow my steak
Hath come from. I only want my money.

Penelope

Then thou hast not put the Empress up to this?
'Twas my understanding that she was thy
Poison'd dagger, thrust at my heart. When thou
Discover'st a dagger at thy breast,
Thou dost not blame the steel, but the cold and
Cruel hand that wieldeth it.

Genevieve

I tire of repeating myself, so 'twill
Be the last time – I want my money.
Whatever 'tis betwixt thee and the
Empress concerns me not. My business is
With her and her alone. The burden is

Hers to repay, and thou can'st be scourged,
Hang in the gallows and burn in Hell if't
Be a means for the Empress to repay
Me – I care not a bugger-bug for thee.
But no. In answer to thy impertinent
Question – I am not the hand that hath struck
At thee. I am the hand that doth squeeze that
Hand. I am the hand that hath threatened that
Hand that hath threatened thee. Personally,
I do yet hold out hope that she wilt fail
In her attempt to squeeze thee. I know a
Fellow who fancies himself a practitioner
Of certain dark arts who would'st pay handsomely
For the Empress' hands, which I did
Promise to take from her should they come back
To me empty.

Penelope

Thou art a vile and loathsome toad. Hath thee
No reckoning of what thou hast set in motion?

Genevieve

Lady, I care not! I am in the
Business of profit, not charity.
If thou come'st here looking for compassion
Or an apology, thou hast mistaken
The sign on my door for that of a parsonage.

Penelope

I will see thee burn, thou churlish harpy!

Genevieve

I will save thee a place by the fire, thou
Foolish minnow. Swim away now, little

Fish, ere I turn into that roguish shark
That people purport me to be, and solve
All thy problems with one sharp gnashing of
My terrible teeth.

Penelope

Keep thy crooked nose out of my affairs,
Thou unwash'd scoundrel, and I will keep my
Fingers out of thine.

Exit Penelope

Genevieve

Oh, that I had ne'er set eyes on either!
What good is't to own the Empress, if she
Is such a blunt instrument – ye gods! 'Tis
Like trying to cut a chicken with a
Fish! I had for a passing moment thought
She might serve, if not my more material
Ambitions, then diversion. For if there's
Aught I love more than gold, 'tis mischief.
I am an agent of chaos, and were
I the king's fool, I would'st paint my face and
Grin and grin and grin, spilling soup and vomit
On both pauper and king alike. Here in
My station, my hands remain clean and
Occupied, but these are not the only
Hands at my disposal – ha! Soon I may
Add two more to my collection, stupid,
Oafish, useless things that they were, attached
To that guts-griping gudgeon, unable
To even perform a simple bit of
Treachery without signing her name all
Over the evidence. Fie on't! It doth
Make my head swim. I shall make haste to speak

With this Inspector, Gadgette. There may yet
Be made a spectacle worth watching
Salvaged from this shipwreck the Empress hath made.

Exit Genevieve

Scene III

A café, where Helena sits with Penelope, drowning their sorrows in chocolate and caffeine.

Penelope

They hath, in truth, evidence to convict
Me, Helena, and I have no recourse
But to hope for miracles or mercy.

Helena

At this very moment, dear Countess, I
Fear I believe in neither. Looking at
The facts, I say without trace of doubt that
I could convict thee. A swaddling babe coulds't
Convict thee. How hath this happened? Dids't thou
Take leave of thy senses? Tell me true – did'st
Thou pawn thy reason for another pair
Of thy damn-ed stryp-ed stockings? Surely
Thou know'st how this looks – you, the
Officer of Finance, writing scrips to

Thine ownself.

Penelope

'Twas all agreed by committee, for thrift's
Sake, to allow me to reimburse myself.

Helena

Thrift! Thrift! Engage not in thrift when the matter
Is the gold of others. Thrift is best
Employed by planning a wedding shortly
After a funeral, that the funeral
Baked meats might coldly furnish forth the
Wedding table.[9] Thrift is the shortcut that
Hath landed many a good man at the
End of the rope – a short drop and a sharp
Stop, heed my words.

Penelope

All is explained in my ledger.

Helena

Which hath disappeared.

Penelope

Which the Empress hath stolen, I'm sure of't.

Helena

But cannot prove. Perhaps 'twere better 'tis
Lost. Without the book, 'twould seem that the only
Evidence the Inspector hast is the

---

[9] Hamlet, Act II Scene I, William Shakespeare

Accusation of the Empress. Should she
Turn up, book in her claw-like hands, and hath
Altered it to suit her needs – thou art good
And truly fuck'd.

Penelope

Perhaps not. The Inspector is not blind,
And doth recognize the smell of fish. He
Hath not only listened to me, but
Truly heard my words. When he hath spoken
To me of his unfortunate duty,
'Twere clear to me that the words left a
Bitter taste in his mouth.

Helena

A man of excellent senses, to be
Sure, but to the point, dost thou think'st he
Believed thee?

Penelope

'Tis possible. But he also made it
Clear that 'tis possible I am a liar.
I am the one on review, and unless
I can cast doubt on the accusations
Of the Empress, I fear I will burn for
This, for the fire hast already been sparked
And is hungry for fresh tinder.

Helena

This doth produce in me a most unsettling
Violence and the seed of my mind grows
Thorny thoughts indeed: choking, poisonous
Vines that threaten all other beauty in

The garden of my imagination.
If the Empress can'st not be reckoned with
In a peaceful manner, I fear more
Drastic measures may be needed.

Penelope

Genevieve is the root and she is an
Unruly weed that must be stomped out if
She cannot be sated.

Helena

Weeds so rarely are. Murder then? Dost thou
Suggest poison?

Penelope

I thought no such thing!

Helena

I hath read – though where I know not – that 'tis
Possible to mix certain concoctions
As to be completely undetectable
By even the most delicate palate.

Penelope

Helena!

Helena

You're right, of course, darling. Only a lowly
Snake would resort to secret poison. Are
You adverse to the sight of blood?

Penelope

Thou art mad.

Helena

Aye, thou speak'st true! In madness I hath good
Claudia slain! The Empress is dead, long
Live the Empress! Pray you forgive the mess.
'Tis like unto that raucous song by the
American minstrel Iggy Pop –
I dost desire to be thy dog. Oh, wilt
Thou let me be thy mad dog, Countess?

Penelope

I think thou dost truly foam at the mouth.

Helena

'Tis only my cappuccino. Hath I
A moustache?

Penelope

Lick thy lips, thou frothy, ill-nurtured lout.

Helena

Better? Am I once more a vision of
Loveliness and angelic beauty?

Penelope

Thy face is much improved, 'tis true, though
Angelic beauty might'st be asking too
Much for such as thee.

Helena

Scullion!

Penelope

Mulder-on!

Helena

Mulder-on? What is't thou call'st me?

Penelope

Lady, I know not. I pray thee indulge
Thy favourite niece in a momentary
Exercise in neologism for
The sake of jest. I'truth, I was caught up
In the moment. I want to believe that
The truth will be brought to light.

Helena

The truth, 'tis out there – scullion. But look
Ye – 'tis that flirtatious young messenger.
Methink'st he hath found thee passing fair.

Penelope

'Twas thy undergarments he coveted
A glimpse of, dear aunt.

Helena

He hath excellent taste.

Penelope

Doth thou wish to discover if he indeed
Tastes excellent?

Helena

Don't tempt me, Frodo! That is, Penelope!
As thou know'st (for thou did'st bear witness)
I am, of late, a married woman, and
Take my pleasure in my husband alone.

Penelope

I beg thee do not embarrass me, nor
Make lewd jests at my expense. He approacheth.

Enter Yorrick

Yorrick

Fine tidings to your ladyships! 'Tis fair
Weather today, as it must be whene'er
Thou dost grace the air with thy gracious forms.

Helena

'Tis an overabundance of grace.

Penelope

Truly. Take care thou dost not trip on thy
Fumbled words, sirrah.

Yorrick

Many thanks to you, lady. I will, as
Thou say'st, take care.

Penelope

What hast thou done, sirrah, to be sent to
Prison hither?

Yorrick

Prison, lady?

Penelope

Yes. Arcadia's a prison –

You

Good God, art thou serious? Hast thou no
Shame at all? Why not purloin the garden
Scene from Romeo and Juliet? Or
The funeral scene from Julius Caesar?
Oh pardon me, thou bleeding piece of earth....[10]
Et tu, Helena?

Helena

Stop, I do beg thee! My most humble
Apologies, darlings, but my niece, the
Dear Countess of Arcadia was, no
Doubt, about to launch into the 'Denmark's
A prison' scene from Hamlet, and whilst it
Is indeed quite brilliant, with that whole
"I could be bounded in a nutshell and
Count myself a king of infinite space,
Were it not that I have bad dreams"[11] line, I
Must interject, lest we divert too far

---

[10] Julius Caesar, Act III Scene I, William Shakespeare
[11] Hamlet, Act II Scene II, William Shakespeare

And end up reciting the whole. In truth,
I cannot bear to see poor Guildenstern
And Rosencrantz lose their heads once more.
I confess I did find them a welcome
Diversion and their deaths pointless and cruel.
Instead, let us use all this talk of prison
As a segue into Penelope's
Pitiable predicament.

Yorrick

Segue, eh? I once had a dog named
Segue. Speaking of dogs, how doth that mongrel
Bitch the Empress?

Penelope

Breathing still, but not on my account.

Helena

I hath offered to put an end to her
Hideous breath, but the Countess hath too
Kind a heart.

Yorrick

Verily, methink'st the Empress would not
Reciprocate in kind.

Penelope

To chill my drink, I need only move it
To her vicinity. But hast thou more
News from thy lady? Or dost thou merely
Come to stare at the writing upon my
Shirt? Mark me – mine eyes are northward, sirrah.

Yorrick

No lady mine, good Countess. I am my
Own man and sell my services to any
With gold to pay.

Penelope

Thou shameless strumpet! Methink'st thou truly
Art a fool at heart and woulds't do well to
Discover some skill at juggling or biting
The heads off chickens, for thy wit doth leave
Much to desire. But I think 'tis not my
Wits thou desires't. Take me not for a
Starry-eyed flirt-gilly. Thou'rt not the
First man who hath sent his eyes out on
Expedition only to have them lost
In the sea of my breasts. Send thee not a
Rescue party; I assure you they are
Truly gone, and 'twould be wise to avoid
These tempestuous waters, for here be
Dragons, I promise thee.

Yorrck

My lady, I would never…

Penelope

Would'st thou not? Pity. I was warming to thee.

Helena

Stop tormenting the boy, Penelope!
What is't thou hast for my lady?

Yorrick

I bring word from Gadgette, a careful
Missive for my lady's eyes alone. I
Pray thou pardon me, good lady, but 'twere
My instruction that the Countess receive
This and no other.

Penelope

Very well, sirrah. Give it to me and
Darken my visage no more. Thou art too
Much i'the sun.

Yorrick

My life is not all sunshine, my lady.
It doth rain at times and when it do, 'tis
Best to be prepared.

Penelope

Speak plainly or hold thy clacking tongue.

Yorrick

'Tis customary to receive a
Gratuity, my lady.

Penelope

Very good. Thou may'st have this one for free –
Grow a beard. Thy eyes do speak of lusty
Passions but the rest of thy face is like
A babe's and I desire'st only to
Pinch thy cheeks and pat thy bottom to move
Thee along. Thou'rt the furthest from
My fantastical imaginations

As is the Empress herself. Grow'st thou
A beard before I see'st thee next.

Yorrick

Good, my lady. *(Aside)* I woulds't have taken a
Bit of coin as well.

Exit Yorrick

Helena

Thou art an incorrigible rascal.

Penelope

I truly am.

Helena

What is't he hath sent thee, good Countess. Keep
Me not in suspense.

Penelope

'Tis an invitation. I am to meet
With the good Inspector, away from
Prying eyes. *(Reading)* "The arithmetic is poor
Indeed and doth lead me to believe there
Is aught else at play here."

Helena

Mathematics never was thy strength.

Penelope

I believe he speak'st of the whole, not the

Contents of my ledger, which hath now been
Discovered.

Helena

I would say 'twere excellent news, but for
The look on thy face.

Penelope

'Tis as I've feared. *(Reading)* "Thy ledger hath, as if
By magic, found its way back to the shelf
Where it hath slept peacefully until lately.
Good Beatrice did, in fair obedience,
Deliver it to me, whereupon I
Did examine its contents only to
Find that all numbers hath fled their pages
Like fleas from a dying dog."

Helena

That contemptible ratsbane!

Penelope

Perhaps not. For are her actions not
Expected? Are they not so transparent
As to be disbeliv'd? As I have told
Thee, this Inspector is no fool.

Helena

Thou think'st he doth call a meeting with thee
To discover the truth by other means?

Penelope

Or perhaps he doth wish to woo me with

Fine wine and mutton.

Helena

My, but thou dost favour thyself mightily
Today, darling!

Penelope

What would'st thou have me say? I feel lucky.
Were I a cardsharp, I would bet my house
And heart. The Empress hath o'erplayed her hand
And hath acted like a villain to the
Very word. A cowardly cur, she hath
Spread the blame everywhere but at her own feet.
She dost protest o'ermuch and hath surely
Drawn the suspicious gaze of all that hath
Their wits about them. No evidence
Exists that doth show my skill in accounting
Nor praises my excellence in book-keeping.
But the mountain of evidence that
Declares her villainy doth waver and
Sway and threaten to topple. If I am
Right (and I am always right)'twill not be
My lack of proof that doth count, but the utter
And obvious destruction of it that
Doth turn the Inspector in my favour.
Come with me, I beg. I do mightily
Desire that thou dost witness this. For if't
Not go well, I will have great need of thee.
Let me not to the gallows go, please say.
I am far too pretty to die today.

Exeunt

ACT III

Scene I

A city street. Genevieve hath been following the Inspector, waiting for an opportunity to bump into him, as if by accident. The Inspector, Gadgette, hath seen her from the very beginning, and is both annoyed and amused at her attempt at subterfuge.

Gadgette

Madam, how can'st I be of service?

Genevieve

Dost thou know me, sir?

Gadgette

Merry! Thou art a spinster!

Genevieve

Not I, my lord. My mother hath, i'truth,

Spun the yarn, but I myself never had the skill.

Gadgette

No, I never forget a face. Truly
Thou art a spinster and thy dry and
Loveless lips hath spun many a yarn.

Genevieve

Dost thou mock me, sir? Surely thou know'st my name.

Gadgette

By thy face, thou art a shoemaker's daughter,
For thy leathery skin doth betray thee.
How oft' dids't thy father tan thy hide? Was't
The lime that hath given thee such a
Sour disposition?

Genevieve

Thou hast taken me for another, I fear.

Gadgette

A candlemaker, then. For thou hast a
Stare like smoke-stunned honeybees whilst they are
Being robbed of their comb. Doth it sting thee
When thou see'st thy waxy gaze staring dully
Back at thee in the looking glass?

Genevieve

Doth thy reflection frighten thee, my lord?
Doth thy conscious prick thee or hath thee
Become a regular attendant of
The apothecary, or perhaps the

Local alehouse? Dost thou drown out the cries
Of the innocents thou hast sent to the
Neck-stretcher?

Gadgette

Ah, thou truly art a spinner of yarns!
Perhaps thou wilt make me a purse for what
Few coins I've left after thou hast pick'd my
Pocket. What can'st I do for thee, Genevieve?
Thou hast made quite a show of hiding thyself
From me, but I tire of this game. Speak
Plainly, I am a busy man.

Genevieve

How fares thy investigation? I am
Eager to have the matter settled, one
Way or the other.

Gadgette

What know'st thou of it?

Genevieve

The money owed me, good my lord, is the
Very matter in question.

Gadgette

And yet thy name hath not come up in my
Investigation.

Genevieve

Until this moment, my lord. Until this
Moment. Ask thyself – why is't the Empress

Is so eager to re-acquire what she
Hath told you are missing funds? For truly,
If it is as she hath said, and young
Penelope hast misappropriated
The Society coin, then the Empress,
Being responsible for the Countess,
Would'st surely bear a modicum of guilt
As well. And yet, I'd bet a fortune the
Empress hath not offered herself up as
Co-defendant.

Gadgette

But who would match that purse? It astounds me,
Truly, how she doth still hold grasp on her power.

Genevieve

A shaky grasp, I assure thee. If her
Hands be claws, they are dull and broken. 'Twould
Take but a tug to pull whate'er power
She doth hold out of her flimsy grip.

Gadgette

And dost thou covet that power? Is that
The final scene in thy grand design?

Genevieve

Ye gods, no! I know well where the heads of
Unloved ministers do spend their final
Days. I've no illusions, I know what scant
Love the gentry bear me and I like my
Head where 'tis. It doth complement my fair
Shoulders quite well. But Claudia, she hath
Nothing without what little power she
Does possess, and she hast shown that she will

Do whate'er it takes to keep it – even
Use thee as her tool, her weapon. For if
She doth succeed in crushing the Countess,
Who would dare stand against her? I care not
A fat tick who is't that takes her place, but
Claudia cannot remain. But not I.
I've no designs on power. It is too
Messy and unreliable. I'll keep
To my gold, if it please thee. As I told
The Empress and that dewy-eyed greenhorn
Penelope – I just want my money.
Or if not, then I'll take my price in trade.
But one way or the other, I will
Balance my accounts.

Gadgette

I would see all scores settled. The Empress
Hath played both the minstrel and the lyre.
She hath plucked the strings of my heart, every
Dissonant note a bitter lie. Each
Sharp-tongued accusation fell flat upon
Inspection. Whispering her treacherous
Melodies in my ears, such hollow toneless
Music as I've never heard before
Nor care to hear again. Lies! Treachery!
Deceit! Injustice! She hath made a
Mockery of my station and a
Perversion of the truth. She hath thrown an
Innocent, beaten and bloodied, to the
Wolves and, God forgive me, this wolf would have
Devoured her, had not reason prevailed.
Come, I have called a meeting. I have sent
For both Penelope and the Empress.
I would'st have thee there, to witness how she
Mewls; how she dodges, deflects and misdirects.
I shall force her to speak with that wicked

Tongue of hers. It shall wag and wag until
It hath loosened itself enough, and when
She hath vomited all her poison and her lies,
I shall use that foolish tongue to hang her.

Exeunt

Scene II

Office of the Inspector. Penelope and Gadgette sit across from each other at a table covered with notes and reports, most specifically, Penelope's ledger.

Gadgette

Long have I considered the facts I have before me,
Checking and double-checking until my mind is sore.
Whil'st my heart doth truly want to believe thee,
My duty to the law doth demand that I have more.
Were I not bound, I'd tell thee what I think is clear –
These papers do paint a picture as drawn by a child.
This bit of villainy is the rankest work of an amateur;
'Tis indeed a tale told by an idiot, a story to be reviled.
This puzzle I did'st try to mend had but one missing part
And lo! When I did'st have need, it did magically vanish,
To reappear with its revealed truth and thine so far apart,
Clearly telling me 'tis thee, dear Countess, I should banish.
Yet the yarn is woven so plain and perfect that I mistrust.
My heart doth ache at the thought of something so unjust.

Penelope

I thank thee, Inspector, for thy honesty
And candor. Is there naught I can'st do, no
Witness I can call?

Gadgette

How did'st thou fare with Genevieve?

Penelope

She bears me no ill.

Gadgette

That sounds promising.

Penelope

Nay, nor love, neither. She careth not
Whether I live or die, but that she gets
Her money.

Gadgette

She hath told me the same.

Penelope

She hath spoken to thee?

Gadgette

Aye, lady, and I hath convinced her to
Accompany me here today.

Penelope

To what end?

Gadgette

This coat of mine is wondrous big and spacious.
In particular the sleeves, up which
I have been known to keep many
Curious things.

Penelope

Thou art a cheeky rogue, I'll give it thee.
Hath Genevieve said naught else?

Gadgette

This whole badly drawn affair rests on the
Debt owed by the Empress to Genevieve.
The Empress hath accus-ed thee of
Mismanaging the Society coin.
If't be true, then the debt falls to thee, and
If't be true, lady, I promise thee, thy
Fate is better in my hands than those of that
Craven fiend Genevieve.

Penelope

Thou know'st 'tis not true.

Gadgette

I believ'st 'tis not true. But what I
Can prove, 'tis another story, one which
I will surely be called upon to relate
To my superiors, who have no
Knowledge of thee or thy predicament.

Penelope

Will they not see motive in the Empress'
Desperation?

Gadgette

'Tis the only thing that doth, at this moment,
Save thee from the rope. The Empress doth
Require the money to pay Genevieve.
That she has it not matters not to
Genevieve. She will have her money or
She will be satisfied.

Penelope

Am I to pay this debt then? Will gold make
All this go away?

Gadgette

Sadly, methink'st that would verily be
Thy salvation indeed.

Penelope

'Tis extortion!

Gadgette

Indeed, Countess. But 'twould satiate that
Wicked beast the Empress, who hath her heart
Set on feeding thee to Genevieve.

Penelope

'Tis unjust!

Gadgette

'Tis an unjust world, Countess. Anyone
Who doth tell thee different likely hath a
Sales pitch for thee.

Penelope

What of my ledger? Thou must surely know
It hath been altered.

Gadgette

If I only had testimony that
'Twas the Empress had last possession of't.

Penelope

Sweet Beatrice! And that goodly rogue Dante.
Surely they wilt –

Gadgette

I hath already considered this, lady.
They wait without. Shall I invite them in?

Penelope

Yes, I beg thee, make haste!

Enter Dante and Beatrice

Beatrice

Good, my lady! How fare thee?

Penelope

I hath, goodly woman, enjoyed better
Days, though I must confess it doth strain my
O'ertaxed imagination to recall
Just when last 'twas.

Dante

There was, my lady, that time when we hath
All had our fill of cheap wine, and stripped off
Our clothes and painted each other's bodies
And ran through the town singing the songs of
Our good lady Lorde.

Penelope

'Twas not I, sirrah.

Beatrice

Nay, nor I. With whom hath thou been cavorting?

Dante

Ah, I now recall – 'twas but a dream, my
Most celestial Beatrice. A nightmarish
Vision, like unto my trip through Hell, and
I was dragged by lusty women – hideous,
Malformed harpies – through the town.

Beatrice

Oh, you poor fellow.

Dante

Thou know'st I love thee.

Beatrice

Thou know'st thou art a terrible liar.

Gadgette

The lady doth not lie, good Dante. Thou
Wear'st thy guilt like a festival mask.
Thou art missing only the devil's horns
To make the impression complete.

Dante

Tell me, sirrah – speak'st I the truth when I
Tell thee that the Empress is a villain
And hath conspired to ruin our good Countess?

Gadgette

Doth thou declare it under threat of
Perjuring thyself and damning thy
Immortal soul?

Dante

Speak not to me of damnation, sir! For
Well I know the fate of perjurers and,
By speaking thus, I fear it not. I've no desire to join
Sinon, that wretched trickster who did with
Guile convince the Trojans to bet on the
Wrong horse. [12]

---

[12] Sinon was an Achaean spy who, in the Aenid by the poet Virgil,
convinced the Trojans that the horse was a gift from the gods, and
that if they moved it into their city, it would protect them. In Dante's
Inferno, Sinon is found in the Eighth Circle, burning forever with a
terrible fever.

Beatrice

'Tis hardly news, Inspector. Surely thou
Dost know thyself she is a villain. 'Tis
Proof of villainy thou seek'st, dost thou not?

Gadgette

I would hear all thou hast to say, lady.

Penelope

Yes, and I, most eagerly!

Beatrice

My lord, I must first confess I hath
Committed a small crime of my own.

Dante

My lady, thou did'st break no just rule.

Beatrice

But we did, my sweet lord, and I pray you
Pardon me.

Dante

Thou did'st, mayhap, stretch some of the good Lord's
Laws, for truly thou did'st perform such acts
That as of yet remain unnamed. But I
Am confident that without precedent,
Thou would'st surely be safe from prosecution.

Beatrice

Oh, thou flatterer!

Dante

I think I hath lost my sin in thee, my
Lady, and do greatly desire to take
It back again in spades. What a cruel,
Inconsiderate apple-john thou must
Think me, to leave my sin in thee.

Beatrice

Thou did'st leave it in me? Thou swore thou dids't
Wear a sheepskin!

Dante

My lady, I was speaking poetically.
I hath meant that I was goodly soft, like
Unto a sheepskin.

Beatrice

Thou paunchy, sheep-biting scoundrel!

Penelope

Please, good Beatrice! Thy tale?

Beatrice

For the love I bear thee, Countess, I will
Continue. For the love I bear thee, Dante,
Thou can'st stew in thy own juices which, thou
Should'st surely know, are not coming within
An inch of me for longer than thou can'st

Conceive or bear. And if I do conceive,
And bear a child, I pray it is a girl,
For any son of thine must surely be
A foolish, preening knave, bent on breaching
Fair maids' breeches and availing himself
Of ale until he is goodly drunk and
Impotent! Go and seek thy hand whil'st I
Tell of what I hath seen.

Exit Dante

Gadgette

Continue, lady, I pray thee.

Beatrice

Dante and I hath found ourselves in
Amorous embrace, though wherefore I know
Not, he is a despicable man.

Penelope

That thou dost love desperately. Please, go on.

Beatrice

And we were in the office, enjoying
Wine and romance, and the spirit did take
Us right then and there, and before long,
We had succumbed to both the passion and
The wine.

Gadgette

You mean –

Beatrice

Right there in the office we did'st fumble
In the dark, until we both hath fallen
Asleep behind an armoire. In the
Darkness, something stirred, it did frighten me.
I carefully sneaked a glance –'twas the sly
Empress I did spy, so stealthily
Returning. And she carried with her the
Ledger I hath given thee.

Gadgette

Why hath thou not told me thus when thou gave'st
The book o'er to me?

Beatrice

I had feared you would chasten thy faithful
Servant for her lewd, unseemly, and
Improper behaviour.

Gadgette

'Tis a lesser crime, surely, than that with
Which I am concerned. I'll hear it spoken
Of no more, only I'll ask thee what I
Hast asked thy husband – art thou willing to
Swear under oath, upon thy immortal soul?

Beatrice

Dante? My husband? Dost thou mock me, sirrah?

Gadgette

Ye gods, woman! Dost thou swear or not?

Beatrice

Aye, I do swear it.

Gadgette

Good. Now go ye and conceal thyself.
I woulds't have thee join the other witnesses
As the Empress hath opportunity
To speak for herself, as thou hast.

Beatrice

Very good, my lord.

Exit Beatrice

Penelope

What think'st thou?

Gadgette

Methink'st there is to be one more bastard
In the world afore long.

Penelope

Nay, Dante is an honourable sort.
And mark not their bickering – 'tis always
Like that with fiery love. What burns most
Fiercely and true and bright doth often singe
The fingers as well. But what think'st thou of
Their testimony?

Gadgette

'Tis fair in my mind, but the real truth shall

Come from the Empress' own lips, I warrant.

Penelope

What dost thou mean?

Gadgette

My sleeves, fair Countess. Remember my
Spacious and clever sleeves. Shall I call in
The Empress? Art thou prepared to face
Thy accuser?

Penelope

Nay, but there is no time like the present.

Gadgette

Art thou certain? I could gift thee with a
Present of time.

Penelope

Thou hath a cunning tongue.

Gadgette

Thou hast nary an idea.

Penelope

Mind it, good sirrah. Thy tongue, that is.
I am grateful, but I am no strumpet.
Let the Empress in. Thou hast been my
Whetstone, and my own tongue is good and
Sharply prepared.

Enter the Empress

Empress

O, Countess, how fare thee? Hath this cruel man
Been threatening thee?

Penelope

He hath been fair and gentle, if but a
Touch familiar.

Empress

'Tis the same with all his sort. Put a
Kindly face and a pair of breasts in front
Of them and they do turn into the
Very image of a gentle lamb.
But such as you and I are not to be
Fooled. We know that underneath, they are but
Wildling wolves.

Penelope

Methink'st 'twould take one wolf to sniff out
Another, thou gibbering, bitch-born scut.

Empress

Dost thou hear how she wounds me!

Gadgette

I brought you both here in the hope that thou
Might'st find resolution in this room; that
Thou would'st speak to each other through me, that I
Might help thee settle this fickle affair
On your own accord.

Empress

(Crying actual tears) She thinks me her enemy! How can'st I
 Convince thee I bear thee no ill will. I
Hath, in fact, fought for thee, defended thee
Against slanderers and cruel back-biters
Who would'st see thee hang for what they assume
Thou art guilty of. I myself, shall
Never believe thou art capable of
The crimes of which they have accused you.

Penelope

I know not this *they* thou speak'st of, Empress.
Is't not thy name on the petition of
Complaint against me?

Empress

Only as a matter of bureaucracy,
Lady, surely thou know'st that. I am
A servant of the people and when the
People speak, I cannot ignore them. Who
Am I that I should go against the
Democratic process?

Gadgette

Who indeed?

Penelope

Then thou deny'st any claim against me?

Empress

I would, dear Countess, but as I hath
Already said, my will is not my own.

Gadgette

Then thou hast no personal stake in this?

Empress

The only personal interest I hath
In this is to get to the heart of the
Matter and learn what hath truly happened
To the money that is unaccounted
For. 'Tis personal because it will break
My heart if 'tis discovered that thou,
Penelope, hast stolen from your
Brothers and sisters of the Society.

Penelope

If thou hast no stake, then why did'st thou steal
My ledger? Thou know'st right well I accounted
For everything in that book.

Empress

Oh, Penelope, thou pitiable
Girl! Is this thy defense? That I hath
Destroyed the evidence that might acquit
Thee? I would'st never!

Gadgette

I have been told otherwise.

Empress

This is pathetic beyond words. I have
No defense for groundless accusations.

Gadgette

The ground doth verily crumble beneath
Thy feet, Empress. Thou wert seen sneak-thieving
In the night like a wanton adulteress
Slipping back into her unsuspecting
Husband's bed.

Empress

And who hath accused me? Was it that
Delusional fool Dante? He who doth
Claim to have gone to Hell and back? Of course,
Were I coupled with that imbecilic,
Onion-eyed sow Beatrice, I would'st long for
Hell most desperately.

Gadgette

Then thou dost deny it?

Penelope

Of course she denies it. Dost thou not hear
Her? Everyone but she is a lying
Knave and she alone doth have the market
On truth.

Empress

Thou desire'st truth? Methink'st thou cannot
Countenance the truth. 'Twas not I who brought
The complaint against thee, truth be finally told.

Penelope

Oh, this do I long to hear! I feared thou
Hast developed a deadly aversion

To veracity, or perhaps even
An allergy to all things factual.

Empress

Can'st we not talk plainly? I did conceal
The truth to protect thee.

Penelope

Thy brand of protection I can'st surely
Do without. 'Tis but paper armour when
I hath need of tempered steel.

Empress

When thou dost hear who thy true enemy
Is, thou wilt not speak so glibly. For the
Wrath of Genevieve is not to be
Taken lightly.

Penelope

As thou thyself know'st.

Empress

I dids't tell thee true, when I said 'twere
Genevieve who hath come to me concerning
A tawdry bit of money. She hath an
Insatiable greed and is as unforgiving
As the devil himself.

Penelope

If we are speaking plainly, then thou know'st
I hath spoken to Genevieve, and
I know thou art indebted to her. I

Know she hath threatened thee.

Empress

Thou know'st nothing, and if thou dost believe
The lies of that foul moneylender, then
Naught I can say wilt convince thee. We are
Both in danger more serious than thy
Innocent mind can conceive – you more than I.
Verily, I hath tried to leave thee out
Of all this, but 'twas Genevieve – surely
She hast a secret hatred for thee.

Penelope

I've done nothing to her. She hath no cause
For hatred, except for hatred's sake
Itself. What yarns art thou spinning now?

Empress

I hath told her our coffers were empty and bare,
That stone doth not bleed, neither doth it grow gold.
She hath whispered with poison, seductive and fair,
That amongst us resided a villain so bold,
A thief who doth smile as she pilfers our purse.
She named thee as the filcher, dear sister , not I,
And I countered her slander with every foul curse.
I hath told her most surely that I had rather die
Than believe thou could'st ever do something so vile.
But the greed of that pinch-fisted miser is boundless.
"I'll have that girl's head," she hath said with a smile,
Though I argued her cruel accusations were groundless.
So you see, 'tis not I who fancies thee dead,
'Tis that harpy Genevieve who doth covet thy head.

Gadgette

I also hath spoken to Genevieve.
It seems all she doth concern herself with
Is the money owed. She hath not mentioned
Our good Countess at all.

Empress

She is harsh and cruel and full of avarice.
In my estimation, 'twere possible
There is no debt at all. Is't not possible
That she hath, with her devious skills, caught
Word that our sister, the honest and careful
Penelope, hath taken leave of her
Position, and did take opportunity
To cast doubt on our Society when
We were most vulnerable and now doth
Try to extort us by putting the dear
Countess under her wicked thumb? Fie! 'Tis
She that is the thief here, sweet sister, not
Thee! Still – someone must pay Genevieve.
For there is a difference between what we
Believe'st – what we even know'st in our hearts
To be true – and what we can'st prove. And the
Villain Genevieve hath made mischief and
Mayhem of the evidence. Someone must
Pay, and much as it doth pain me to say,
Penelope, that burden doth fall on thee.

Enter Genevieve from out of hiding, followed by Dante, Penelope and Helena.

Genevieve

I think'st not, thou deceitful, fly-bitten
Miscreant! Thou art the worst sort of

Prevaricator! Inspector! Bind this
Mewling wretch! I'll have justice most swift and
Immediate for her craven and
Ill-conceived fictions.

Helena

Do what thou wilt, 'tis naught that I hath not
Already considered myself, but hath
Restrained myself for Penelope's sake.

Beatrice

What Hell, good Dante, hath thou said await'st
The Empress? For I grow impatient.

Dante

'Tis not certain, my love. 'Tis possible
She would'st suffer the fate of flatterers,
And spend all eternity immersed in
Excrement. Or 'twould be fitting, perhaps
For her to suffer disease and sickness
Like the perjurers and liars. My choice
Would be the fate of the corrupt.

Beatrice

Ah yes, sweet Dante, thou hast spoken thus
Before. The Eighth Circle of Hell, reserved
For liars, deceivers, and the corrupt.
A lake of boiling pitch was it?

Dante

Thou'rt an astute student, sweet angel.

Beatrice

And thou a captivating teacher.
Perhaps I ought to stay after class and
Thou can'st fill me with all the knowledge
Thou hast at thy disposal.

Dante

How can'st I ignore thy sweet calling – nay,
My noble responsibility to
Educate thee? 'Twould be an offence to
Heaven, lady, and I've seen too much of Hell.

Penelope

There is surely an inn nearby. Go thee
And get a room.

Dante

I'd rather go prepare the pitch and tell
The gath'ring mob that the Empress is no more!

Beatrice

And I shall spread the compost for her. Let
Her lie in the filth of her lies after
Thou hast covered her with pitch.

Exit Dante and Beatrice

Gadgette

Hold! 'Tis Penelope who is't the most
Offended. Vengeance should be hers to take.
Let her speak on't. What say'st thou, good Countess?

Penelope

She is a fool, but I am loathe to kill
Her. Do what thou wilt, only look not to
Me to strike the blow of vengeance.

Genevieve

That right is mine, thou speak'st true. Go on,
I have no quarrel with thee, Penelope.
Only I'll have what I hath come for.
Inspector, draw thy sword. I hath promised
Yon Empress I would'st take her hands and, mark ye,
I am a woman of my word.

Gadgette

And my dogs shall have her lying tongue!

Empress

Thou dost great wickedness this day! The
People! Bring'st me to my people and thou
Wilt see how I am loved. Do this thing and
Thou wilt surely face the wrath of the mob.

Gadgette

I said I'd have thy tongue, thou unmuzzled
Varlet! Thou hast spoken thy final lies!

The Inspector cuts off the Empress' tongue and throws it offstage, where we hear an angry mob cheering.

Genevieve

Stay not thy blade sirrah, until thy work
Is finished. Give me the pox-marked hedge-pig's

Hands, that I might close my account with her.

The Inspector cuts off the Empress' hands and delivers them to Genevieve.

Gadgette

Here is thy prize, thou vicious harpy!
Begone! Else I find some fault in thee, for
Truly thou art no innocent!

Genevieve

And a handsome prize at that. I take my
Leave of thee and forgive thee thy veiled threats,
Just this once.

Exit Genevieve

Helena

Oh wicked day!
My gorge doth rise, yet I shake with righteous glee.
Dear Countess, listen as I say.
She did'st conspire in wickedness to do this unto thee.
Thou'rt truly blameless of all of which thou wert accused,
Whil'st she hath sinn-ed grievously against all present here,
Who now seek equal vengeance for how they were abused.
Look not on her with pity, nay, shed not a precious tear.
In this life, 'tis not often justice is meted out so plain
And oft' the villain doth live to cause ruination on another.
'Tis right for you to feel ill at ease at causing others pain;
Thou'rt a good and kindly girl, as was thy lovely mother.
I pray thy pardon, darling, if this scene you cannot stand,
But punishment is ready and doth wait on my command.

Penelope

I shall take my leave of thee and love thee ever.
I will retire and try to achieve impossible tasks
As are accomplished by only the terribly clever.
Tell them I have gone to mourn, if anybody asks.
But I shall try to forget this night and all those past,
Wherein I did'st cry myself to sleep in frustration.
I'll lock myself away and pray this ugliness can't last.
This I do declare with steely resignation.
If thou hast need of me, thou wilt find me locked away,
Perhaps indulging fantasies of Cummerbund Bandersnatch
And in that sacred, private place of mine I'm sure to stay,
Locked away in solitude behind strong deadbolt and latch.
If thou hast aught that will remove this from my memory,
Be not stingy with thy magic and in haste do give it me.

Gadgette

Be well, Countess. 'Twill all be over soon.

Exit Penelope. Enter Dante and Beatrice

Dante

Come, my lady Claudia! Come let us
Anoint thee with oil, and rub sweet putrescent
Compost in thy wounds, thou charry villain!

The Inspector and Beatrice take the Empress by the arms and drag her off stage, led by Dante. Only Helena remains.

Helena

Behold thy Empress! Empress of filth and lies!
Empress of treachery and deceit.
Whose lies are forever silenced, that

Poisonous tongue torn from her grisly face
And the vile machinations of her cruel
Manipulation, those fat-finger'd hands,
Forever stilled. This gruesome portrait she
Now doth form will stand to illustrate this
Exemplary lesson: Threaten not those
Who enjoy my protection, for if thou
Dost not desire thy life be torn apart,
Tempt not my wrath when't comes to my affection
And harm not those beloved of my heart.

End

Epilogve

"That's not at all what happened," Penny sighed, closing the book. "I really don't think you should print this."

"It's what should have happened," I sighed back, topping up my Greyhound (vodka and grapefruit juice for the uninitiated – I take mine with Ruby Red grapefruit juice, darlings, and I thank you very much).

"I don't wish her any harm," Penny shrugged. "She's a bitch. She'll pull this shit on the wrong person one day, and it'll all come falling down on her."

"Life is not Shakespeare, darling. Real life is full of cruel, manipulative, lying assholes with all the conscience of egg-sucking foxes, and most of the time, we call them successful businessmen. Or politicians."

"Thou art a preening knave, you know that?" Penny said, affecting her very best Elizabethan thespian. "Thou think'st thou art *so* clever."

"I think nothing of the sort," I said. "I'm just glad all the charges were dropped and that I'm not currently visiting you behind glass."

"I look terrible in orange – and not a word about it

being the new black, because that is completely and utterly untrue. You'd never catch Robert Smith or Trent Reznor or any of those boys from My Chemical Romance in orange."

"My Chemical Romance broke up, you know," I said.

"Oh sure, rub it in why don't you? Like my life isn't terrible enough." Penny wailed.

"It's been quite a while now."

"It still hurts, thou insensitive lout!"

"Oh, Penelope, thou art melodrama personified, thou truly art."

"Only when you write it... *darling*. And it's Penny, dammit!"

⁂

Acknowledgements

Thank you to Dr. Seuss, who first sparked in me a love for rhyming verse.

Thank you to my eighth grade teacher – a cruel bastard who had no right teaching children but who nonetheless introduced me to Shakespeare by way of Othello.

Thank you to Kenneth Branagh, whose adaptations, along with some great BBC productions (several of which starred Sir Patrick Stewart, when he wasn't busy playing a comic book character or the Captain of the Starship Enterprise) made my love for Shakespeare deepen.

Thank you to all those who have played Hamlet – except for you, Ethan Hawke – I'm still waiting for an apology for that travesty.

Thank you to Samantha, who helped talk me down while the events this book are based loosely upon were going down. Thank you to Katherine for not killing me for writing this, against every instinct in your body.

I had a little inspiration from pangloss.com when I needed to string together some insults.

Thank you to Martin, Pamela, and Janet for reading and proofreading – what would'st I have done without thee – friends I know not.

Lastly, thank you, darlings. For reading, for demanding more, and for trusting my dabbling in forms somewhat less than of usual fare.

About the Author

The enigmatic Helena Hann-Basquiat dabbles in whatever she can get her hands into just to say that she has.

She's written cookbooks, ten volumes of horrible poetry that she then bound herself in leather she tanned poorly from cows she raised herself and then slaughtered because she was bored with farming.

She has an entire portfolio of macaroni art that she's never shown anyone, because she doesn't think that the general populace or, "the great unwashed masses" as she calls them, would understand the statement she was trying to make with them.

Some people attribute the invention of the Ampersand to her, but she has never made that claim herself.

Last year, she published Memoirs of a Dilettante Volume One, and is publishing Volume Two in the Spring of 2015, both available on Amazon.

Helena writes strange, dark fiction under the name Jessica B. Bell. Find more of her writing at helenahb.com, whoisjessica.com, or connect with her via Twitter @HHBasquiat

Look for VISCERA, a collection of strange tales by Jessica B. Bell to be published by Sirens Call Publications later in 2015.

Illustrations are by Ali Akbar. Contact him at AliAkbar000023@gmail.com for commissions.